God Bless

Meredith Miz

Phil. 4:13

SAVING NIDIA

WRITTEN BY:

MEREDITH THIGPEN

ILLUSTRATIONS BY:

JASON PRUITT

TATE PUBLISHING & Enterprises

Tate Publishing
& Enterprises

Tate Publishing is committed to excellence in the publishing industry. Our staff of highly trained professionals, including editors, graphic designers, and marketing personnel, work together to produce the very finest books available. The company reflects the philosophy established by the founders, based on Psalms 68:11,

"The Lord Gave The Word And Great Was The Company Of Those Who Published It."

If you would like further information, please contact us:
1.888.361.9473 | www.tatepublishing.com
Tate Publishing & Enterprises, LLC | 127 E. Trade Center Terrace
Mustang, Oklahoma 73064 USA

Saving Nidia
Cover design & interior design by Elizabeth Mason
Illlustrations by Jason Pruitt

Published in the United States of America

ISBN: 1-5988681-4-4

06.12.12

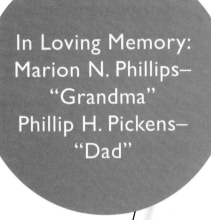

In Loving Memory:
Marion N. Phillips—
"Grandma"
Phillip H. Pickens—
"Dad"

I would like to dedicate
this book to my husband
and my mother.

Without their
encouragement and
support, this book would
still be collecting dust
on my shelf.

~M.T.

May the road rise to meet you
May the wind be always
at your back
May the sun shine warmly
on your face
May the rain fall softly
on your fields
And until we meet again
May God hold you in the palm of
his hand

~Irish Blessing

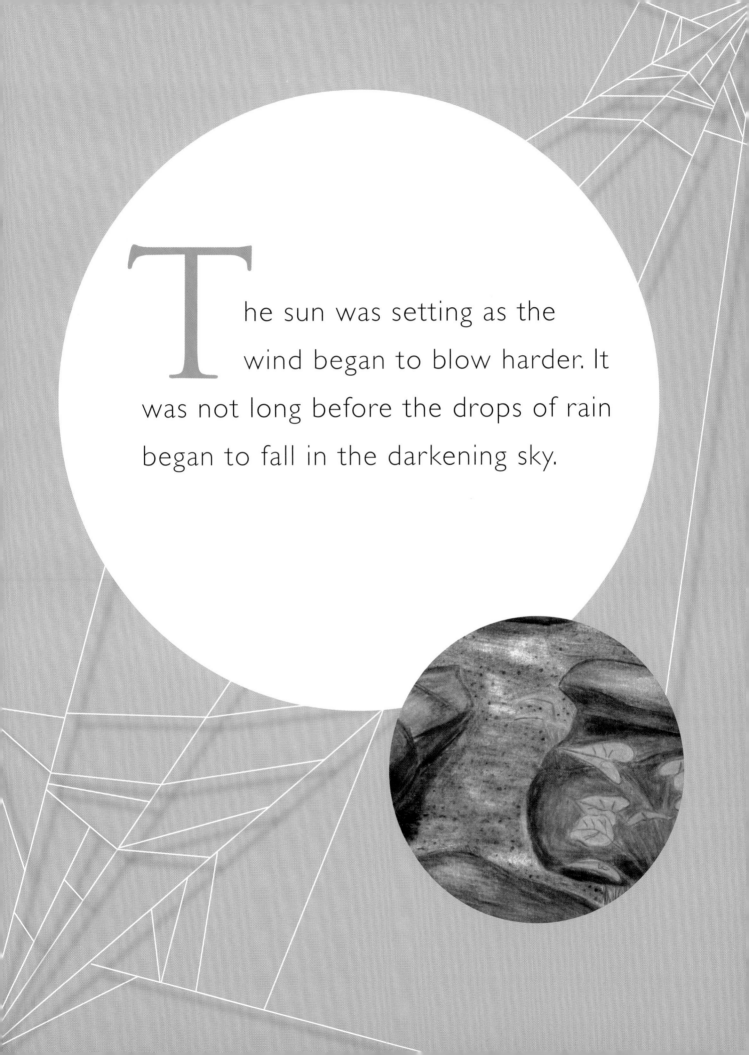

The sun was setting as the wind began to blow harder. It was not long before the drops of rain began to fall in the darkening sky.

The small creature looked nervously out of the root cluster. She knew that it would not be long before the creek next to her home would begin to rise. This had never been a problem before, but instinct told her that this stormy night would be different from storms of the past.

She could not take the chance of being flooded just days before her babies would hatch. She quickly decided to strap them to her back and move to a safer location.

The bank of the creek was steep, but she was determined to reach higher ground. The egg sack was very heavy. She barely made it up to the path that followed alongside the creek.

She spotted the perfect cover on the other side of the path and began to slowly drag the egg sack across. She was almost safe when she suddenly felt the heavy thud of feet coming her way. She braced herself for the common reaction when seeing a spider—

SQUISH!

She felt a strong hand pick her up, but instead of hurting her he covered her from the rain.

This kind stranger seemed to have also been caught in the storm. He found shelter under a small rock overhang and sat down.

"Nidia, it is a very bad night to be carrying around such an important package," the stranger said. "Where were you going?" Exhausted, Nidia answered, "The storm was flooding my home and I am in search of a new home for my children." The stranger looked at her, smiled, and said, "I am also in search of something, Nidia. I am in search of people to show the wonders of my Father's home. So it seems that we are both in search of something important." Nidia, finally feeling safe, fell into a deep sleep.

When she woke the next morning, she found herself in a small, carved wooden home. There was plenty of room for both her and the egg sack, which was already inside. She soon realized that her new friend had made this wonderful home for her. How could she ever repay his kindness?

Nidia crawled out of her home to thank her friend and noticed a large round ring at the top of the house. As she was looking at the ring she heard from behind, "I was hoping you and your children would come with me on my journey. Your family will always be safe with me."

Nidia thought for a moment, then answered, "I would like that very much, but I would first like to know one thing." "What is that?" asked the stranger. "Last night you called me by my name. How did you know my name was Nidia?"

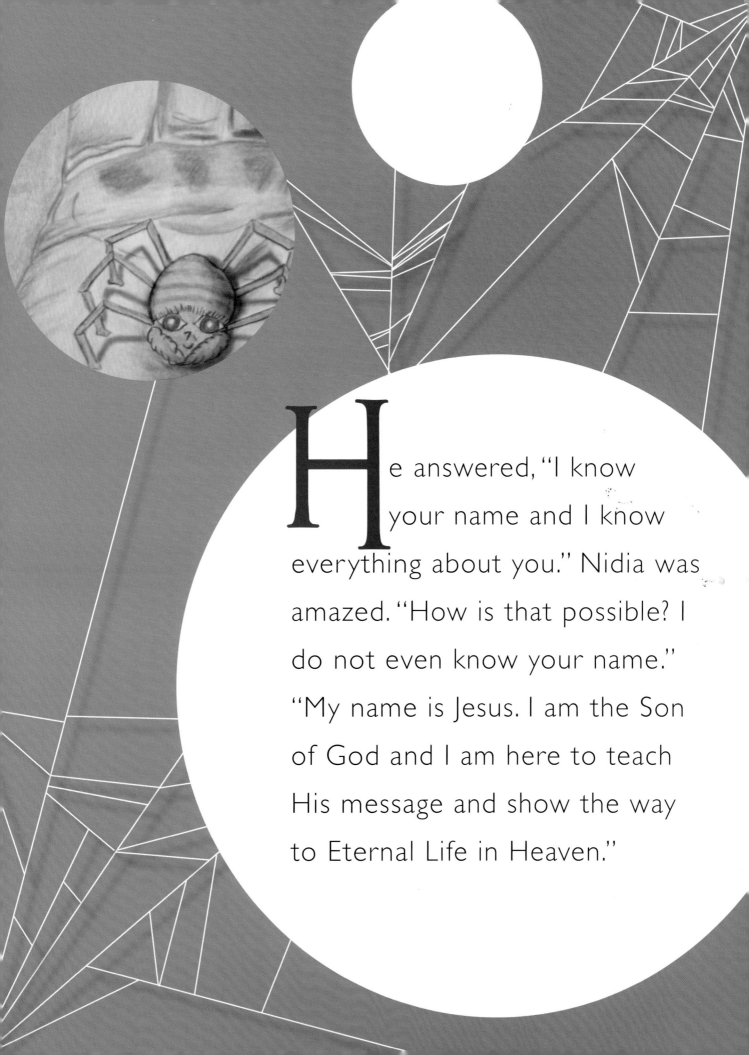

He answered, "I know your name and I know everything about you." Nidia was amazed. "How is that possible? I do not even know your name." "My name is Jesus. I am the Son of God and I am here to teach His message and show the way to Eternal Life in Heaven."

Nidia knew then how she would repay Jesus. "You are a great example for everyone and a wonderful friend. I will accept your gift and I will travel with you. My children will listen to you teach as they grow. When it is time for them to leave me, there will be a great wind that will carry them to far places. Each one will share your message to all of God's kingdom."

Jesus then ran the end of his belt through the round ring at the top of the small wooden house and tied a knot. Nidia and her children had a new home.

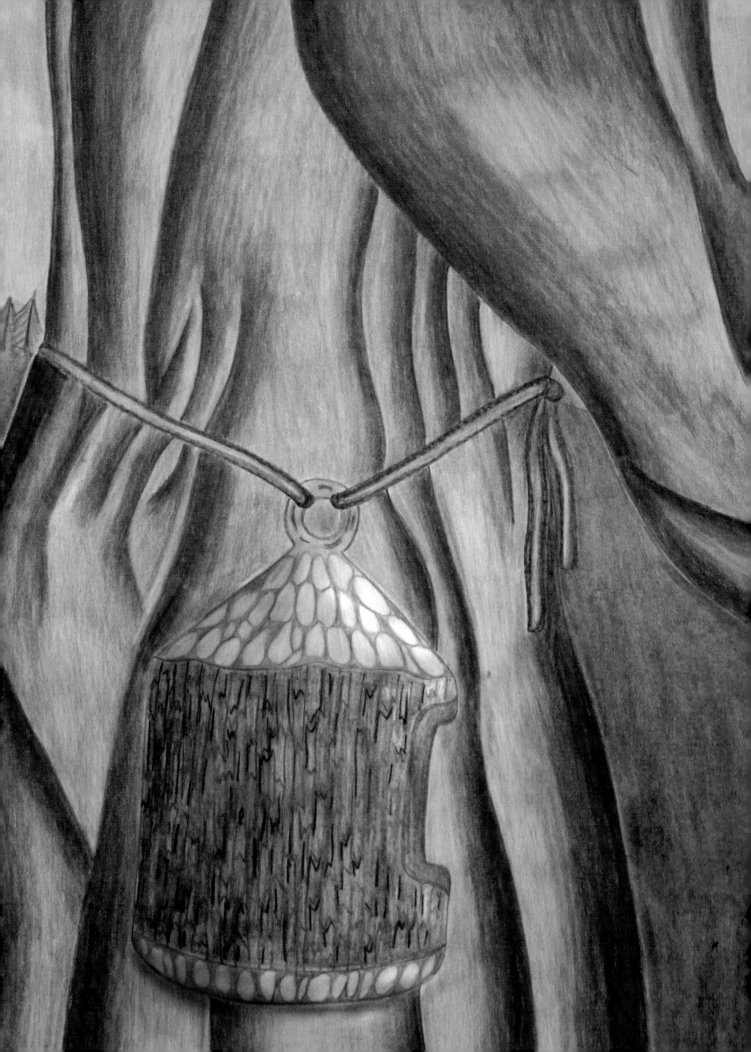

As the sun rose the following morning, the first of Nidia's small spiders found its way out of the egg sack. For some time they filed out of the sack and into their new home.

For the next three months the spider family traveled with Jesus and saw so many wonderful miracles.

They witnessed Jesus' ability to heal the sick and feed the hungry. They also listened carefully to his descriptions of God and Heaven. Jesus was a friend to everyone he met. So many people loved him, but there were many people that doubted him. Jesus knew that his time on Earth was coming to an end.

He called Nidia and the children to gather with him. "Now is the time for us to part ways. I have treasured our friendship and our time together, but God has a different plan for me now. I will miss you all."

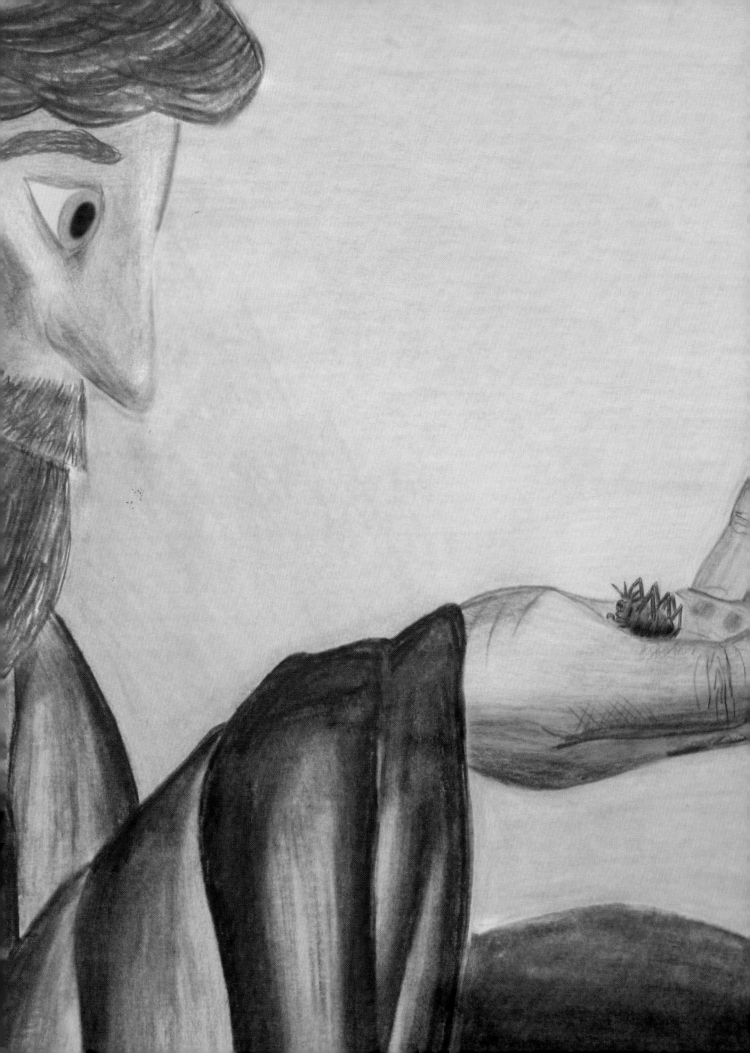

One of the smallest spiders named Zeke spoke up, "Please, take us with you. We do not mind doing something different. We can go wherever you need to go." Jesus looked fondly at his little friend. "This is a path that I must walk alone, but know that I will always be with you in your heart. You will never be alone. Now is the time for you to take my message and spread it to others."

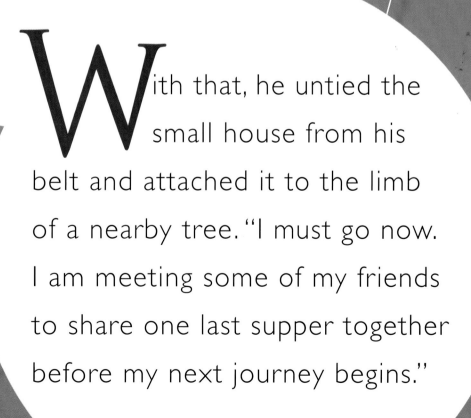

With that, he untied the small house from his belt and attached it to the limb of a nearby tree. "I must go now. I am meeting some of my friends to share one last supper together before my next journey begins."

N idia had been quietly listening, knowing that this day would come.

"Jesus, I must know one last thing. The night we first met, you took care of me instead of hurting me. I am only a small, insignificant spider. Why did you do that?"

"Remember, God created *all* creatures, great *and* small—each with a purpose."

"Thank you for everything, Jesus. It is hard to say goodbye to such a good friend."

"This is not goodbye, only a goodbye for now."

The sun began to set as Nidia watched Jesus walk down the path to his new home.